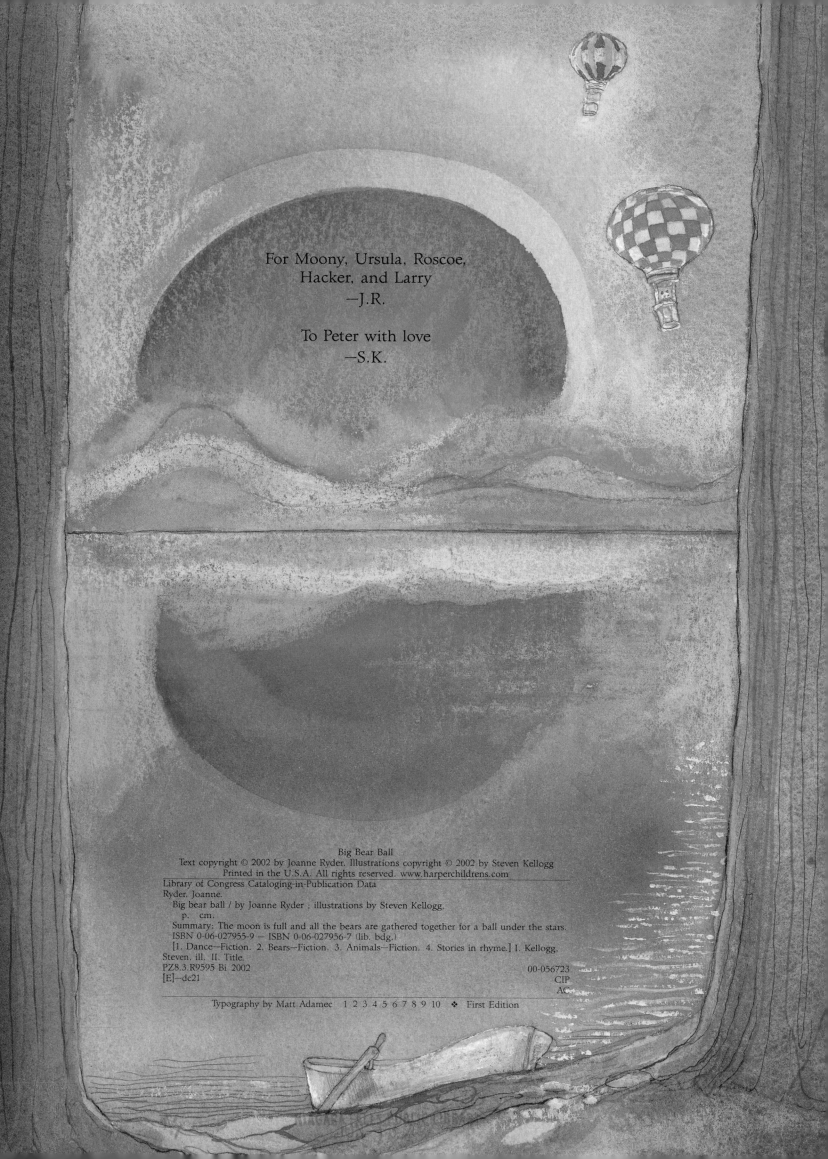

For Moony, Ursula, Roscoe,
Hacker, and Larry
—J.R.

To Peter with love
—S.K.

Big Bear Ball
Text copyright © 2002 by Joanne Ryder. Illustrations copyright © 2002 by Steven Kellogg.
Printed in the U.S.A. All rights reserved. www.harperchildrens.com
Library of Congress Cataloging-in-Publication Data
Ryder, Joanne.
  Big bear ball / by Joanne Ryder ; illustrations by Steven Kellogg.
      p.   cm.
  Summary: The moon is full and all the bears are gathered together for a ball under the stars.
  ISBN 0-06-027955-9 — ISBN 0-06-027956-7 (lib. bdg.)
  [1. Dance—Fiction. 2. Bears—Fiction. 3. Animals—Fiction. 4. Stories in rhyme.] I. Kellogg,
Steven, ill. II. Title.
PZ8.3.R9595 Bi 2002   00-056723
[E]—dc21   CIP
                                                                                  AC

Typography by Matt Adamec   1 2 3 4 5 6 7 8 9 10   ❖   First Edition

BIG BEAR BALL

Joanne Ryder

illustrations by
Steven Kellogg

HarperCollins*Publishers*

Bushes full of berries,
trees full of moon—
bears arriving
by balloon.

A broad-beamed caller
howdys all:
Welcome, friends,
to our Big Bear Ball!

Hey there, Honey Bear!
Don't be shy.
Never been dancing?
Give it a try.
Some bear's eyeing you
with a grin.
Just grab her paw,
and let's begin.

Small bears sway
and slap your paws.
Tall bears stomp
and pop your jaws.

Two paws up,
waving high.
Catch some stars
and scratch the sky.

Now thump those stumps
and wake the moles.

Let's rouse the foxes
from their holes.

Watch that Honey Bear
catch the beat!
Why, who said
he had two left feet?

Now hug your sweetie
and make a chain.
Let's follow the moonlight
down the lane.

The moon will take us
where it will.
Let's shuffle through the meadow
and amble down the hill.

We're heading to the water
where the frogs sing along,
so fiddler, please play
a splish-splash song.

Now all you ladies twirl those frogs,
and all you fellers spin those logs.

Watch out, Honey Bear!
Don't fall in!

WHOOPS!

Well, he met up with a 'gator . . .

. . . and took him for a SPIN.

Happy bears, slappy bears,
wild as they get!
Why, pass the hankies.
Everybody's wet!

Now bow to your partner
and bow to the moon.
Our fiddler will play
a good-night tune.

Go lightly, sprightly,
on your way.
May you dance
with the music
as we welcome the day.

Farewell one!
Farewell all!
See you next full moon
at our Big Bear Ball.